THE FANTASTIC WORLD OF THE

Oddies®

For Tom

Oddies Ltd, 1 Hay Hill, London, W1J 6DH

First Published in Great Britain in 2003 by Oddies Ltd.

ISBN 1-904745-01-6

Printed in Great Britain

THE STORY OF
Footy Oddie

By Grant Slatter and Alex Hallatt

The footballer put his clothes and his favourite pair
of socks into the washing machine.

"Chug chug whirr, chug chug whirr," went the washing machine. Then it did something strange.

It speeded up really fast and there were sparkles and a tinkling sound, then a little 'pop!' Something magical had happened and one of the socks had disappeared.

The missing sock was called Footy and he was off
to Oddieworld for an adventure!

"Wow! I'm finally going to see Oddieworld," he said as he zoomed through space. "The other socks say it's beautiful and sunny."

But when he popped out of the Sockhole into Oddieworld he got a shock - it was raining! Then he heard a soft voice. "My naughty sister, Witchy, is boiling a rain potion."

It was Sock Fairy. "She's making the grass
too muddy to play football on and we need someone
to go to Bad Oddie Island to stop her," she said.

Footy turned to look at Bad Oddie Island.
But when he turned back Sock Fairy had disappeared,
leaving a shiny new football in her place.

"I suppose I'd better try to get to
Bad Oddie Island," said Footy. Then he set
off, kicking the ball along with him.

Down on the beach Footy saw Sid, the Sailor Oddie. "Ahoy there, could you take me to Bad Oddie Island?" he said.

They were sailing along when suddenly
there was a big splash next to the boat.

"Was that a whale?" said Footy. "No!" said Sid.
"It was a cannon ball from that pirate ship, look out!"

"Stop that, will you?" shouted Footy.

" I'm trying to get to Bad Oddie Island so I can stop all this rain."

"Oh are you?" said the Captain Pirate Oddie. "Well, since it's making our gunpowder soggy, we'll let you go this time."

Soon they arrived on Bad Oddie Island.
Litterbug Oddie was dropping rubbish nearby.
"Do you know where Witchy is?" asked Footy.

"She's up there on top of the muddy hill, guarding her pot," replied Litterbug. "But you won't be able to reach her because it's too slippery."

She was right, it was too slippery for Footy to climb. "If only I could knock over that pot," he said.

Then he had a brilliant idea.

He popped his football up into the air...

...and kicked it really hard.

BAF!

It hit Witchy's pot and there was a big bang as the pot exploded.

Witchy screeched as she slid all the way down
the slope. Then she flew off into the woods.

The rain stopped and out came the Sun.
"Thanks for your help Footy," said a familiar voice.

It was Sock Fairy. "We'd love you to stay in Oddieworld for ever!" she said. "But I'll magic you back if you really want me to." And what do you think Footy did?

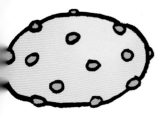

He chose to go back. "I'll have to go home because it's the cup final on Saturday," he explained, "but can we have a game of football to celebrate first?"

So they did!

Bad Oddies v Good Oddies.

And guess who scored two goals?

When it was time to go home, Sock Fairy made a magic Sockhole appear. "Goodbye everyone," said Footy. "See you all again soon, I hope."

Then he closed his eyes and leapt in!

The washing machine made a tinkling sound
and a little 'pop!'

...Footie was back home.

CUT OUT AND COLOUR IN

GROWN-UPS CUT HERE

THE FANTASTIC WORLD OF THE Oddies®

CUT OUT AND COLOUR IN

GROWN-UPS CUT HERE

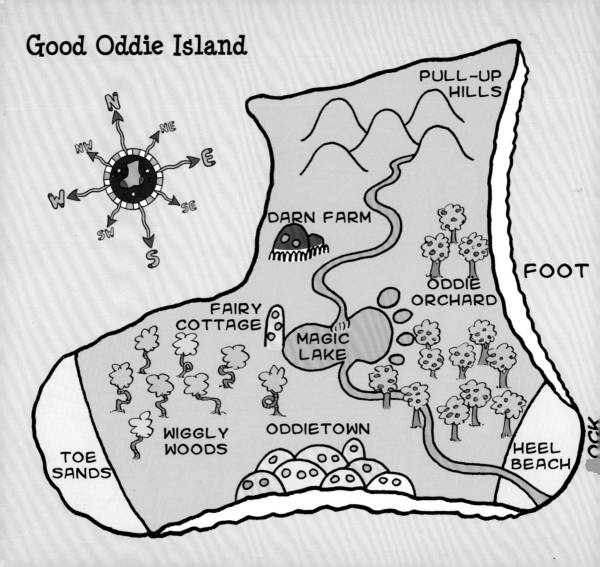